Traction Man

is Hero

MINI GR

RED FOX

Traction Man is here!
(Wearing Combat Boots,
Battle Pants and his
Warfare Shirt.)

Traction Man is guarding some toast.

Now
who's going to help
with the washing up?

LOVELY
FLAKES

He has volunteered for a Special Mission.

Traction Man is diving in the foamy waters
of the Sink (wearing his Sub-Aqua Suit,
Fluorescent Flippers and Infra-Red Mask).

He is searching for the
Lost Wreck of the Sieve.

"Well done,
Scrubbing Brush!
You can be my pet!"

Traction Man is crawling through the overgrown shrubbery near the Pond, wearing Jungle Pants, Camouflage Vest, and Sweaty Bandanna.

The Dollies have all been buried up to their waists in the Flower Bed by Wicked Professor Spade.

"Oh, Traction Man, how can we repay you?"
"Think nothing of it, Ladies.
    All in a day's work."

Traction Man and Scrubbing Brush are **deep, deep** down at the Bottom of the Bath. (Traction Man is wearing his Deep-Sea Diving Suit, Brass Helmet and Metal Shoes.)

Somewhere down here, legend says, are the Mysterious Toes.

Oh no! The Toes have suddenly appeared and have grabbed **Scrubbing Brush!**

"No Mysterious Toes are stealing away with my brave Pet! **Take that! And that!**"

The Toes cannot **stand** it and give back Scrubbing Brush.

Traction Man takes some photographs of the Mysterious Toes.

Traction Man and Scrubbing Brush are in the Giant InterGalactic People Mover.

They are counting Christmas trees.

They are put into suspended animation for some of the journey.

At last!
Granny's!

Oh! How lovely.
An all-in-one knitted green romper suit
and matching bonnet!

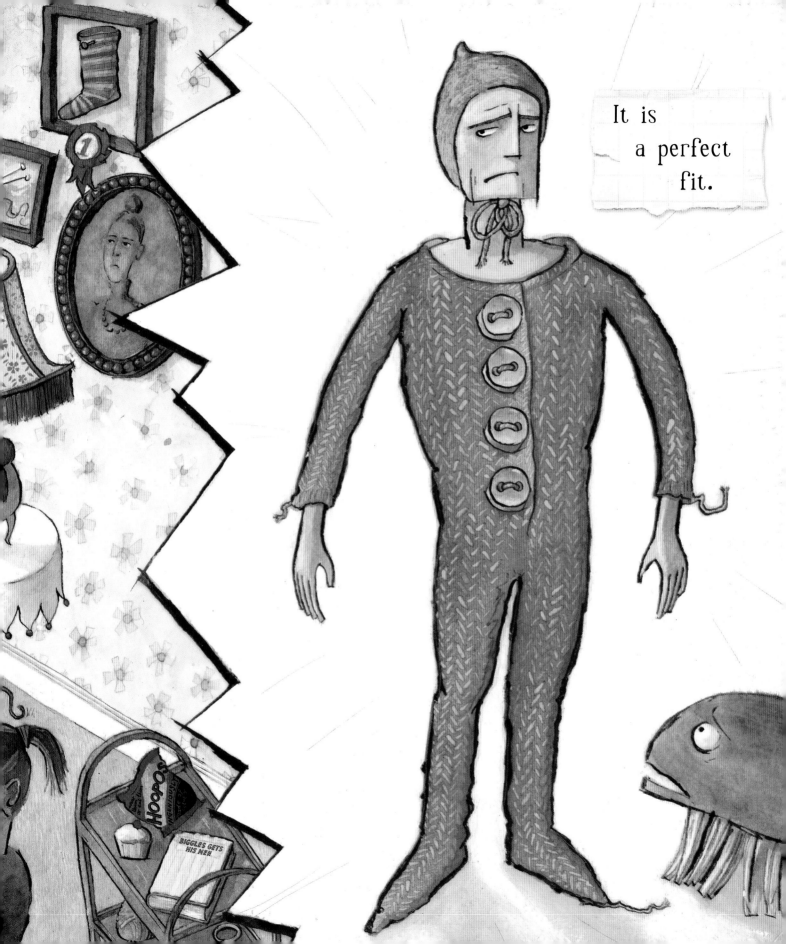

It is
a perfect
fit.

Traction Man is speeding in his **Supersonic Space-Cup** and **Saucer** (wearing his all-in-one knitted green romper suit and matching bonnet) on his way to rescue the Cupcake from the clutches of Doctor Sock.

But—
Oh no!

Well at least Scrubbing Brush doesn't laugh at him.

Traction Man is sitting on the edge of the Kitchen Cliff
(wearing an all-in-one knitted green romper suit
and matching bonnet).

Arf   Arf   Arf.

Arf!

Arf!

Arf!

Oh **DO** be quiet,
Scrubbing Brush.

My Goodness! Down there!
 All those spoons have crashed! They must be helped –
but how? The Kitchen Cliff is very high.

Traction Man and Scrubbing Brush
are relaxing after their latest mission,
lying comfortably on a book
in the huge blue expanse
of the Carpet.

Traction Man is wearing his
knitted Green Swimming Pants
and matching Swimming Bonnet.

They are both wearing their medals.

And they know they are ready
for Anything.

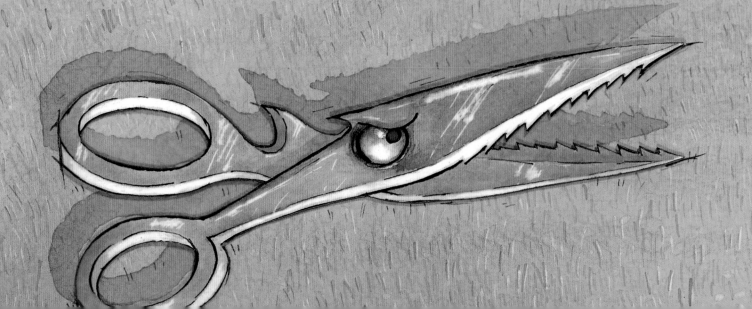

To my
big brother
TONY

More fabulous picture books
from Mini Grey:

EGG DROP
THE PEA AND THE PRINCESS
BISCUIT BEAR
THE ADVENTURES OF THE DISH AND THE SPOON

TRACTION MAN IS HERE
A RED FOX BOOK 978 0 099 45109 9

First published in Great Britain by Jonathan Cape,
an imprint of Random House Children's Books
A Random House Group Company

Jonathan Cape edition published 2005
Red Fox edition published 2006

7 9 10 8

Copyright © Mini Grey, 2005

Red Fox Books are published by Random House Children's Books,
61-63 Uxbridge Road, London W5 5SA

www.kidsatrandomhouse.co.uk
www.rbooks.co.uk

Addresses for companies within The Random House Group Limited
can be found at: www.randomhouse.co.uk/offices.htm

THE RANDOM HOUSE GROUP Limited Reg. No. 954009

A CIP catalogue record for this book is available from the British Library.

Printed in Singapore